LIGHTNING BOLT BOOKS™

Meet a Baby Kangaroo

Anna Leigh

Lerner Publications ◆ Minneapolis

For Eli

Lerner Publications Company
A division of Lerner Publishing Group, Inc.
241 First Avenue North
Minneapolis, MN 55401 USA

For reading levels and more information, look up this title at www.lernerbooks.com.

Library of Congress Cataloging-in-Publication Data

Names: Leigh, Anna, author.
Title: Meet a baby kangaroo / Anna Leigh.
Description: Minneapolis : Lerner Publications, [2017] | Series: Lightning bolt books. Baby Australian animals | Includes bibliographical references and index.
Identifiers: LCCN 2016037260 (print) | LCCN 2016050317 (ebook) | ISBN 9781512433845 (lb : alk. paper) | ISBN 9781512450552 (eb pdf)
Subjects: LCSH: Red kangaroo—Infancy—Juvenile literature. | Red kangaroo—Life cycles—Juvenile literature. | CYAC: Kangaroos.
Classification: LCC QL737.M35 L444 2017 (print) | LCC QL737.M35 (ebook) | DDC 599.2/223—dc23

LC record available at https://lccn.loc.gov/2016037260

Manufactured in the United States of America
2-52502-23890-1/21/2022

Table of Contents

Brand-New Baby

This red kangaroo is about to give birth! Her baby has been growing inside her for almost one month.

There are several kinds of kangaroos, but red kangaroos are one of the most common.

When the baby arrives, it is about the size of a jelly bean. Its eyes and most of its body are not yet developed. But its forelimbs are strong. The baby will continue to grow inside its mother's pouch.

A baby kangaroo is called a joey.

The joey uses its forelimbs to climb up its mother's furry belly to reach her pouch. It must make its journey all alone. The joey uses its sense of smell to find its way to the pouch.

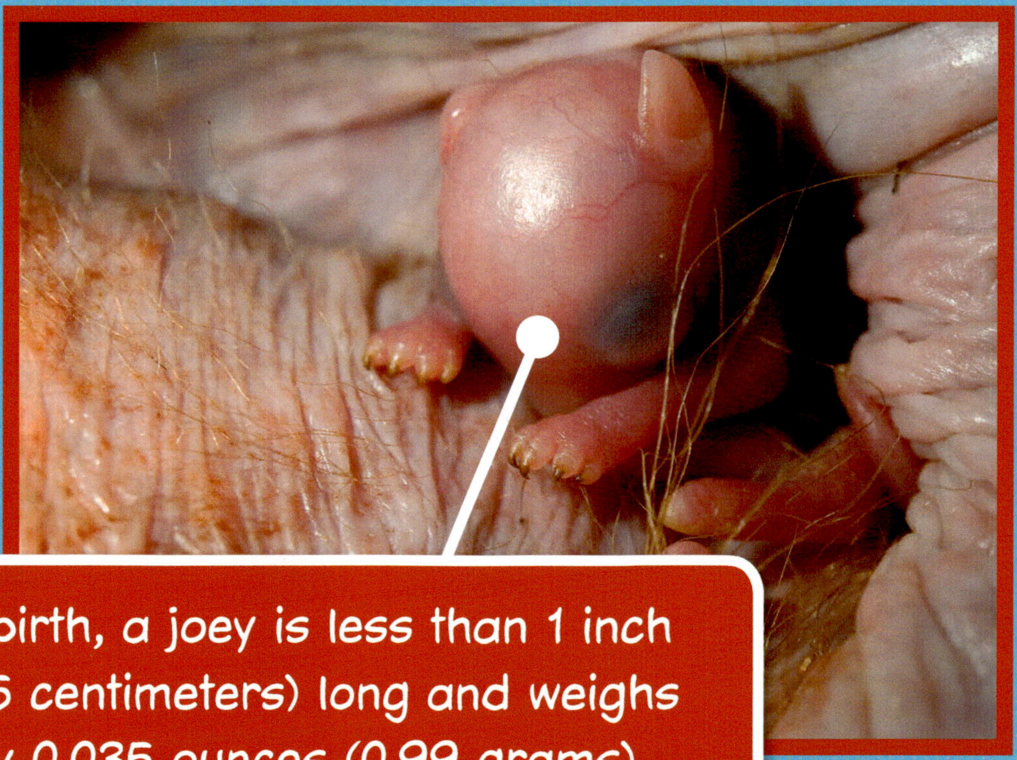

At birth, a joey is less than 1 inch (2.5 centimeters) long and weighs only 0.035 ounces (0.99 grams).

It takes less than five minutes for the joey to reach its mother's pouch. It latches onto her teat and begins to drink milk.

Mom and Joey

The joey stays inside the pouch for the next six months. Its back legs grow stronger, and it begins to grow hair.

A joey's eyes open after about one hundred days.

After about six months, the joey is big enough to leave the pouch. At first, it stays out for only a few minutes. Then it jumps back into the pouch headfirst.

The mother kangaroo stamps her foot to warn the joey of danger when it's outside the pouch.

When the joey is eight months old, its mother stops letting it back inside the pouch. Soon she will have another joey.

A mother kangaroo may have one joey in the pouch, one out of the pouch, and another baby growing inside of her!

The joey still isn't ready to leave its mother. It stays close to her while it learns to be part of the group of kangaroos.

Grazing and Chewing

A joey drinks milk from its mother for one year. It may be too big to climb into the pouch now. But it still sticks its head inside to drink.

The young kangaroo starts eating grass when it is eight months old. Kangaroos spend most of their time grazing on grass and other plants. Their bodies take in water from the plants too. Kangaroos can go four months without drinking water!

The kangaroo has to chew and swallow its food twice to digest the tough plants. This is called chewing cud. Sheep and cows are other animals that chew cud.

Did you know kangaroos had something in common with sheep and cows?

Kangaroos have special teeth to help them eat grass. Their sharp front teeth cut the grass, and their back molars grind it up.

A kangaroo's molars wear down often. They fall out, and the kangaroo grows new ones.

All Grown Up

Male kangaroos are fully grown after about two years. Then they will leave their mothers and join a new mob.

An adult male kangaroo can weigh 200 pounds (91 kilograms) and be 6 feet (2 meters) tall.

Females usually stay with their mother's mob.

Females are fully grown when they are sixteen to twenty months old. But they aren't ready to have their own joeys until they are two years old.

This young kangaroo will have her own joeys someday.

Kangaroos often wander around large areas to find food. But Australia gets very hot, so kangaroos rest in the shade during the day and move around and eat at night.

Kangaroos dig holes in the dirt and lick their fur to keep cool.

Kangaroos may live for up to twenty-two years. New red kangaroo joeys continue to be born, so the kangaroo's life cycle goes on!

Kangaroo Life Cycle

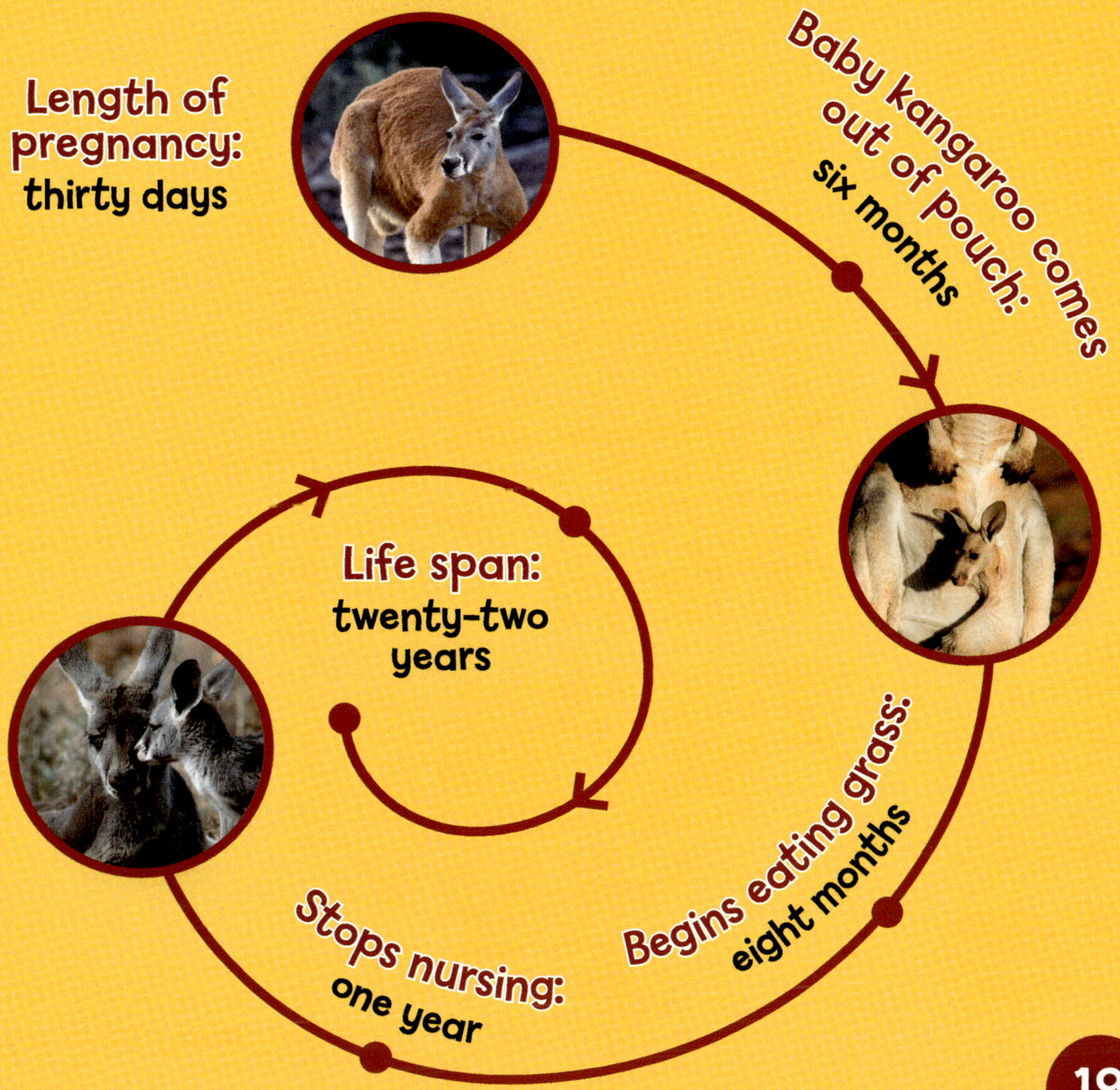

Habitat in Focus

- Wild kangaroos live only in Australia. They roam through its desert and grassland habitats.
- Female kangaroos are able to have babies at any time of the year. But if there isn't enough water, a female will not give birth.
- Sheep farms are common in Australia. Kangaroos and sheep often share the same grazing lands and water sources.

Fun Facts

- Red kangaroos can hop as fast as 35 miles (56 kilometers) per hour. Their average hopping speed is 12 miles (19 km) per hour.
- Only male red kangaroos have reddish hair. Female red kangaroos have blue-gray hair.
- Male kangaroos are sometimes called boomers, jacks, or bucks. Females are called does, flyers, or jills.

Glossary

cud: food that an animal brings back up from its stomach into its mouth to be chewed again

digest: to break down food

forelimb: an arm or leg at the top or front of the body

molar: a large tooth near the back of the jaw

teat: the part of a female animal through which her young drink milk

Further Reading

Active Wild: Kangaroo Information
http://www.activewild.com/kangaroo-information-and-facts-for-kids

Lawrence, Ellen. *A Kangaroo's Life*. New York: Bearport, 2012.

National Geographic Kids: Kangaroo
http://kids.nationalgeographic.com/animals/kangaroo/#kangaroo-hopping.jpg

Owings, Lisa. *From Joey to Kangaroo*. Minneapolis: Lerner Publications, 2017.

Saxby, Claire. *Big Red Kangaroo*. Somerville, MA: Candlewick, 2015.

Index

Photo Acknowledgments

The images in this book are used with the permission of: © blickwinkel/Alamy, pp. 2, 14; © Frans Lanting Studio/Alamy, p. 4; © Mitsuaki Iwago/Minden Pictures, pp. 5, 7, 8; © Ardea/Steve Downer/Animals Animals, p. 6; © Jurgen and Christine Sohns/Minden Pictures, pp. 9, 17; © Theo Alfos/Minden Pictures, p. 10; © Steve Christo/Corbis/Getty Images, p. 11; © Helene Ecker/Animals Animals, p. 12; © Werner Layer/Animals Animals, p. 13; © Juniors Bildarchiv GmbH/Alamy, p. 15; © Yva Momatiuk and John Eastcot/Minden Pictures, p. 16; © Ardea/John Paul Ferrero/Animals Animals, p. 18; © Dave Watts/Alamy, p. 19 (top); © Theo Allo/Minden Pictures, p. 19 (middle); © Owen Newman/Minden Pictures, p. 19 (bottom); © LOOK Die Bildagentur der Fotografen GmbH/Alamy, p. 20; © imageBROKER/Alamy, p. 22.

Front cover: © John White Photos/Alamy.

Main body text set in Billy Infant regular 28/36. Typeface provided by SparkType.